next stop grand central

8 10
9 11

THANK S TO AND NANCY PAULSEN FOR CHARLOTTE SHEEDY BEING SUPER DUPER

THANKS TO COLLEEN HALL AND ALL AT TO SARAHOROWITZ FOR MAKING THIS VERY NICE PROJECT HAPPEN

SPECIAL THANKS TO PATRICIA RALEY AND ALL THE GRAND PEOPLE AT GRAND CENTRAL

Library of Con

ISBN 1-878811-869-0-876

A lit ext set in Bodoni.

New York Designed by M + Co

IT'S ALWAYS
NICE TO MAKE
A GOOD
IMPRESSION

next stop

GRAND CENTRAL

...gress Catalog Card Number 98-25135 CIP data available if you really want it but I'm sure you have better things to do. Right... object and lovely destination... character and mysterious... some delicious... ways... because there was a... have never been bored... Egypt and Israel and... trips in India and... Have taken... PUFFIN BOOKS... New York... 10014. THis edition published by Puffin Books, 2004. Published simultaneously in Canada Printed in China. So Long.

by
Maira Kalman

Dedicated (as always) to T.K. LBK and ATDOMLK!

Puffin Books,
New York.

Singing trees.

Green birds.

The snappy new day is here. You might wake up
and play with your dog, Pete.
You might
build a chair
out of sticks,
or chew
some gum.

You might do
nothing
at
all.

But

while
you
are
sitting
there,
there is a place
in New York City that
is the busiest, fastest, biggest
place there is.
It is a train station.
This place is called
Grand Central.

One day you might (you must) go there.

It's not called grand for nothing!
Everything about it is grand! huge! **monumental!**
Grand staircases.
Polished marble floors.
Stupendous star-filled
ceilings.

Don't take
my picture

Every
day 500,000
people walk, run,
dash, rush—criss-crossing
on and off trains.
It is such a madhouse, people say
IT'S LIKE GRAND CENTRAL IN HERE!
How does it work?
Who does what?
What does
who?

It is 5:30 a.m. While you are dreaming about a giant One-eyed squid,

Lenny Maglione is at his desk. He is in charge of the building. He has 316 people working to make sure the building doesn't fall down. He can see everything from his window onto the main concourse.

STAY ALERT

Roberto is a carpenter.
He fixes doors that need to
open *and* close.

Bob and Steve work the scissor lift —
lifting objects heavier than a **potato** (let's say).

Ed
changes
one of
the **kazillion**
light bulbs,
standing on
a very tall
scissor lift.

(Mel Schmeklen is just
hanging around watching)

Etha delivers the mail —
a letter
to Mr.
Pickle
cannot
go to Mr.
Schnikle.

if you have a complaint —
too hot, too cold, too silly —
you complain to Wanda.
She hears 100
complaints a week.
Could you hear that
many complaints
and always be
polite? She is.

A place has to be safe. From no-goodniks. From fires.

George Coppola
is the chief of police.
He eats a **tuna** sandwich for lunch

with Bob Hennessey,
the fire chief
(who prefers a grilled **cheese** sandwich).

Let's say twelve children Empire State Building from Mamaroneck, on their way to the get separated from their teacher, Mrs. Sauerkraut.

Help!

The policemen and women and the firemen and
women will rush to their aid.
The teacher will be found. The children will be happy
(except for Arthur Beanstalk who is not crazy about Mrs. Sauerkraut).

You can't have a train station without trains. Every day 548 trains come and go.

Dave Schanoes makes sure they are on time, safe, working – not broken! Sometimes an unexpected situation happens. Then there is an emergency meeting in the Situation Room. Here is a situation:

I am not chicken

if

you and your
best friend Gus are
on the 10:40
to Rye Playland
(yippee!!)!
and a giant chicken is on the track
blocking the train, Dave can call that chicken
and convince him logically to get off the tracks.

The Ferris wheel is waiting.

The trains work so people can work. And live.

Ethel Schloogle is going to the Venus Beauty Salon for a haircut (good luck!).

Napoleon Noble is going to act on Broadway.

Edith and Selma are going to the Metropolitan to see a painting by Tintoretto.

The Oblensky twins are going to their tap dancing class in Carnegie Hall.

The woman with the blue pancake hat is going to Chinatown to buy Poo Nik Tea.

Little Ofir Weiss is going to the Bronx Zoo.

Sidney Salmon
is going
to play
chess
with his
cousin Zoltan Zizmore.

The fezman
in the fez
is going
skating
in Central
Park.

I love pancakes

The man in the
flat red pancake hat
is going to eat pancakes at
Joe Jr's Coffee Shop.

Pete is
on his way
to Riverdale
to cheer up
Ida Frumkiss.

Fred
Farfel is heading
to Tuckahoe
where he
will stub
his **toe**.

Mrs.
Millicent
Bluebird
is
bringing
a
rare
lemon
to
the
lemon
man
at
the
Botanical
Gardens.

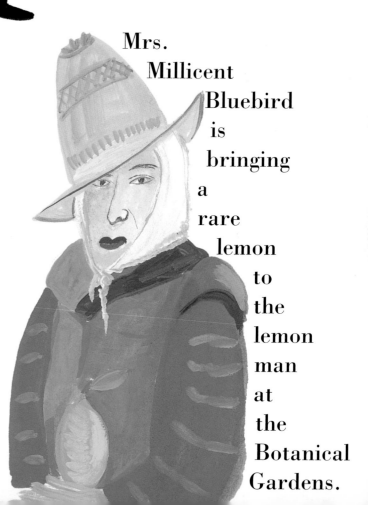

People are starting to get hungry. They race to eat. Some people say, AHOTDOGANDFRIES ANDMAKEITSNAPPY!

105 TRACK 106

give me a bite please

A man
in a porkpie hat
buys cherry pies.

A woman named
Minna Fuchsbaum
says,

"This lolli pop is delicious!"

FISH IS BRAIN FOOD

Hi, New England

Hi, Manhattan

At the Oyster Bar you must sit at the counter and watch Marino Marino make oyster stew. He adds 3 shakes of paprika to the stew.

When he is not
making stew,
Marino thinks of interesting
math problems like this...

2 black shoes

+

a fish-eyed man wearing
2 black suspenders

+

an angry stickman wearing
1 black hat (with pompoms)

+

1 brown dog named Elvis

=

5 black things that
you can wear and
1 brown thing
that will bite
you if you
try to wear it

I can't find
my yo-yo

It's time to catch a train. If you have a question you go to Audrey in the information booth under the big clock. She can't tell you where your lost **yo-yo** is, but she can tell you where to catch the 10:27 to Valhalla, the 2:20 to Dobbs Ferry, the 4:14 to Cos Cob… but don't catch a cold!

At the ticket window you must buy a ticket (unless you are a **dog** who rides for **free**) from Robert. You can't buy a ticket to Po-DUNK, Pensi-COLA, or Pe-ORIA (because these trains don't go there), but you can go to Westport, White Plains, or Williams Bridge.

Some people travel light. With a toothbrush and a book.

Some people carry 14 suitcases, a piano, skis
and a goldfish named Leopold.
Then Melvin Johnson will help you get to the train.
He would prefer you travel light.
He does.

The trains don't drive themselves.
Mary Donch is the engineer. She puts on yellow gloves and blue safety goggles and takes a big brass key out of her pocket and turns on the train. She can drive up to 90 miles an hour. She drives up a storm, but safely. She can go backwards too.

DON'T TICKLE THE ENGINEER Thank You

GO GO GO GO GO GO

KEY

HORN

I love my fish

FISH

PAIL

DON'T EVER TOUCH THIS BUTTON →

OR SOMETHING HORRIBLE WILL HAPPEN

Thank You

BOOK

DOG

Walking down the aisle is the conductor. Not of the orchestra, of the train. Robert takes out his hole punch and punches your ticket. If you have an emergency, like your knee itches, tell him. He is in charge. He will know what to do. (Scratch it!)

This is the hole punch. Every conductor has a different punch with their personal punch shape.

ANDY'S PUNCH

JEFF'S PUNCH

BILL'S PUNCH

TRUDY'S PUNCH

HAWAIIAN PUNCH

Woof

This is
the room
of all
importance.

Mr. Frank
Chidester
runs the
Lost and Found.
If you lose a red button,
or a suitcase full of diamonds,
or your false teeth,
chances are Mr. Chidester
will have them.
Most lost things
don't bark, but
once...

...once
the absent
minded
Mrs. Clarence
Pffafenburger was
bringing her show dog
Mitzi from Darien
to Greenwich for a
tea party. When
Mrs. Pffafenburger
got off at Greenwich,
she realized
to her horror
that she
had left
Mitzi on
the train.

Good bye Mitzi

But not for long.
Mr. Chidester found Mitzi
and sent her home.
On her own private train.

Things you will see in Grand Central.

Someone waiting patiently.

Someone waiting impatiently.

A very on time clock.

Two triangles and a bee.

Someone looking up.

Someone looking down.

Someone sleeping.

A peppy dog named Elvis.

Three gruesome gargoyles.

Someone rushing…

really rushing…

… really really rushing!!!
(it's called rush hour after all)

Things you won't see.

Einstein sailing.

Boris
Pasternak
pouring
a drink for his
wife, Zinaida.

The silver
bucket
in his dream.

A boy named Will dreaming on a red book.

The pyramids
of Giza. (That's
another trip.)

It's **6:00** p.m. In Vanderbilt Hall…
(It was Mr. Vanderbilt who had the place
built in 1903 after all)… there is a lively celebration going on.
The singer Olga Shmedvig is
singing. When she hits her
high notes people think
it is the train whistle
and start running
for the train.

"my kne eee"

Herbert Moosehump is having fun and so is little Ervin Pil who will grow up to be a famous scientist because he eats beets every day!

this is fascinating

It's dinner time.
(People are always hungry.)

Someone
orders frogs' legs
and root beer.

I lost my
yo-yo

Oh no
darling

The place never stops,
because people work
all
night
long.

Dr. Beautyman
is going to
Roosevelt Hospital
to deliver
the Krupchik triplets
(good luck Krupchiks!).

Mel Bongo
is going to bake
600 jelly doughnuts
at Georgie's Bakery
on 125th St.

Sal Monkfish
is going home after
playing in the orchestra.

Simon LaSkunk is
going to Dover Plains to
stare at the sky.

Suki
Matsumoto
is going home
after a long
longer longest poetry
reading by Simon LaSkunk.

Zagwat Holstein is
going to his
newspaper
job.

Greg is the night station master.

He has a walkie talkie.

Ralph brushes famously.

Albert
sweeps
swimmingly.

Great googamoogas! It's 5:30 a.m.
While you are dreaming
of turning your piano teacher
into **a frog,**
Lenny Maglione is back
at work again.
And that's how it goes.

Lenore
protects
positively.

Ed checks electricity
enthusiastically.

Trains are **trips.**   And trips are **adventures.**

And adventures are

new ideas

and

Romance

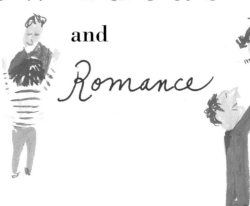

and you can't ever know

what in the world

will happen

which is **exactly**

why

you are going.

And *kisses,*

kisses,

k i s s e s

are always there.

I love
you Mimi

"Hello Hello. I'm so glad to see you."

"It's been toooo long."

"You've grown **so very much.**"

"Good-bye."

"Good-bye."

"I love you."

"I'll miss you."

"Don't forget to write."

"Don't catch a cold."

"Be careful, darling."

"I love you."

"Good-bye."